Please return or renew this item before the latest date shown below *m₁ ⏐ D*

1 0 JUN 2014

– 9 OCT 2014

2 4 OCT 2014

Thank you for using your library

THE BATMAN STRIKES!

Raintree is an imprint of Capstone Global Library Limited, a company incorporated in England and Wales having its registered office at 7 Pilgrim Street, London, EC4V 6LB - Registered company number: 6695582

First published by Raintree in 2014
The moral rights of the proprietor have been asserted.

Originally published by DC Comics in the US in single magazine form as The Batman Strikes! #3.
Copyright © 2014 DC Comics. All Rights Reserved.

Ashley C. Andersen Zantop *Publisher*
Michael Dahl *Editorial Director*
Sean Tulien *Editor*
Heather Kindseth *Creative Director*
Bob Lentz *Designer*
Kathy McColley *Production Specialist*

DC COMICS

Joan Hilty & Harvey Richards *Original U.S. Editors*
Jeff Matsuda & Dave McCaig *Cover Artists*

ISBN 978 1 406 27963 4

Printed in China by Nordica
0214/CAZ1400346
17 16 15 14
10 9 8 7 6 5 4 3 2

British Library Cataloguing in Publication Data
A full catalogue record for this book is available from the British Library.

JOKER'S WILD!

BILL MATHENY ....WRITER
CHRISTOPHER JONES ....PENCILLER
TERRY BEATTY.......................................INKER
HEROIC AGE.......................................COLOURIST
PAT BROSSEAU ....LETTERER

**BATMAN CREATED BY
BOB KANE**

HEY YA, HEY YAAAA... ♪ ♫

...YA YA YA... HMM. PERHAPS I'M ENJOYING MASTER BRUCE'S KARAOKE MACHINE A LITTLE TOO MUCH.

SHWOOM

MASTER BRUCE? IS THAT YOU?

AHEM. I DON'T RECALL HEARING THE DOORBELL!

CHILL, OLD MAN, OR I'LL BUST A CAP IN THAT SHINY SUIT OF YOURS!

FEEL LIKE DROPPING THE GLOVES AND GOING A ROUND OR TWO, POPS?

OUTLAW *And* DISORDER

BILL MATHENY
WRITER

CHRISTOPHER JONES
PENCILLER

TERRY BEATTY
INKER

PAT BROSSEAU
LETTERER

HEROIC AGE
COLORIST

HARVEY RICHARDS
ASST. EDITOR

JOAN HILTY
EDITOR

BATMAN CREATED BY BOB KANE

6

PINK TWO LIPS BAR

THEY SAY THAT THE *BOSS* IS TAKING MEETINGS TONIGHT AT THE *CHORTLE PORTAL.*

AND HE'S PAYING SERIOUS MONEY TO *NEW RECRUITS.* YOU IN?

SOLD.

WHERE DO I GO TO BREAK OFF MY PIECE?

YOU AIN'T GOING NOWHERE, NEW GUY. *UNDERSTAND?*

WHACK

YOU BETTER GET THAT NOSE LOOKED AT. *UNDERSTAND?*

YOU'RE *DEFINITELY* IN.

LET'S GO.

THIS IS YIN. THEY'RE ON THE *MOVE.*

WORLD FAMOUS CHORTLE PORT...

EXCUSE ME, *MR. KARD...*

I WAS *SO UGLY* WHEN I WAS A KID THAT EVERY TIME I LOOKED IN THE MIRROR, MY RE-FLECTION COVERED HIS EYES!

...SOME PEOPLE ARE HERE TO SEE YOU.

EXIT

3,794 ITEMS ON THE MENU AND STILL *NO POTATO SKINS.* GREAT.

PLEASED TO MEET YOU.

LIKEWISE...

WORLD FAMOUS CHORTLE PORTAL

YIIII!

FZZZT

WHOOPS-- FORGOT WHAT I WAS WEARING. IT'S THE ONLY THING I'VE FOUND THAT STOPS ME FROM PICKING MY NOSE!

HA HA HA HA HA

HAVE A SLICE OF *PIE*, MY TREAT.

BETTER YET, TAKE THE WHOLE THING--

SPLAT

HA HA HA HA HA HA HA

--IT'LL PUT SOME *CHUCKLE* IN YOUR *BUCKLE!*

HA HA HA HA HA

SEE HERE--I'M LOOKING TO HIRE THE *BEST*. BUT IT'S SERIOUS BUSINESS. WE'RE NOT TALKING *WHOOPEE CUSHIONS* AND *FAKE BARF*...

WHOOPIEE

CHORTLE PORTAL LAFF LOUNGE

FREEZE! GOTHAM P.D.!

≥GASP!≤ JUST LOOK AT HIM--*BLOWN AWAY* BY MY *GENEROSITY!*

BZZZT! THAT WAS WEAK. *GAME OVER, BATMAN!*

CHONK

OH, POOH.

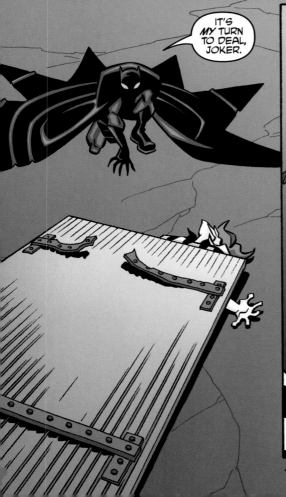

IT'S MY TURN TO DEAL, JOKER.

OUCH... "*MY TURN TO DEAL.*" HAHAHAHA! YOU *KILL* ME, BATMAN...

YOU *PARTY POOPER!* THEY MATCHED MY *EYES!*

PTING

MY FATHER GAVE MY MOTHER THIS NECKLACE ON THEIR FIRST ANNIVERSARY.

I WRAPPED THE BOX. IT WAS A WONDERFUL EVENING.

LOVE AND MEMORIES, SIR. THOSE ARE LIFE'S *TRUE* PRECIOUS GEMS.

I WONDER WHAT THEY'D SAY ABOUT WHAT I'M DOING NOW. I MEAN, YOU HAVE TO BE KIND OF CRAZY TO... YOU KNOW. RIGHT?

PERHAPS I COULD INTEREST YOU IN A GAME OF CARDS. WITH *JOKER'S WILD*, OF COURSE.

ALFRED, EVERY TIME I LOOK AT THIS, I THINK ABOUT HOLDING HER HAND.

A LOADED QUESTION, SIR. *STUBBORN*, YES. DEFINITELY *DETERMINED* AND *DEDICATED*. BUT *CRAZY?* I THINK NOT.

NO WAY. A TENNIS MATCH? AND THIS TIME I'LL WIN!

THAT, YOUNG MR. WAYNE, MAY BE THE CRAZIEST THING YOU'VE EVER SAID.

24

END

CREATORS

BILL MATHENY WRITER
Along with comics such as THE BATMAN STRIKES, Bill Matheny has written for TV series including KRYPTO THE SUPERDOG, WHERE'S WALDO, A PUP NAMED SCOOBY-DOO, and many others.

CHRISTOPHER JONES PENCILLER
Christopher Jones is an artist who has worked for DC Comics, Image, Malibu, Caliber, and Sundragon Comics.

TERRY BEATTY INKER
Terry Beatty has inked THE BATMAN STRIKES! and BATMAN: THE BRAVE AND THE BOLD as well as several other DC Comics graphic novels.

GLOSSARY

bonding closely connecting with someone

circuits complete paths that electrical currents can flow around

competitive closely contested

concussion injury to the brain caused by head trauma

dedicated if you are dedicated, you give a lot of time and energy to something

determined if you are determined to do something, you've made a firm decision to do it

generosity the practice of being giving

lame weak or unconvincing

likewise also, or in the same way

precious rare and valuable, or very special

recruit individual who has recently joined a group

scramble to mix up

secure safe, firmly closed, or well protected

VISUAL QUESTIONS & PROMPTS

1. In order to show that the Joker is singing in these panels, the artists included music notes next to the text. What are some other ways they could have shown that Joker was singing?

2. Joker likes making puns, or words that have two meanings. Identify the two words in these two panels that are puns.

3. In this panel, we see the card the Joker has thrown crossing over the borders of the other panels. How does this effect make you feel when you read it? Why do you think the artists chose to illustrate it this way?

4. In this spread, the artists used different panel borders than on the other spreads. What are these panel borders, and why do you think the artists chose to depict them in this way?

READ THEM ALL!

THE BATMAN STRIKES!

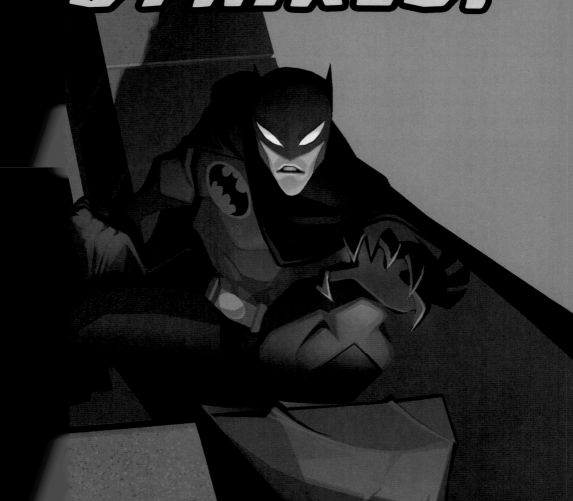